When Rapunzel meets Flynn Rider, the pair travel across the kimgdom. To find out what happens read along with me in your book. You will know it's time to turn the page when you hear this sound.
Let's begin now.

Narrator: Cindy Robinson
Mother Gothel: Donna Murphy
Rapunzel: Mandy Moore
Flynn Rider: Zachary Levi
Captain of the Guard: M.C. Gainey
Hook Hand Thug: Brad Garrett
Producers: Ted Kryczko and Jeff Sheridan
Additional engineering: Frank Trube

Incantation [#6] (Healing)
Performed by Mandy Moore as "Rapunzel"
Music by Alan Menken and Lyrics by Glenn Slater
© 2010 Wonderland Music Company, Inc. (BMI)/Walt Disney Music Company (ASCAP)

First published by Parragon in 2012
Parragon
Queen Street House
4 Queen Street
Bath BA1 1HE, UK

Disney PRINCESS

Tangled

PaRRagon

Bath • New York • Singapore • Hong Kong • Cologne • Delhi
Melbourne • Amsterdam • Johannesburg • Shenzhen

$\mathcal{O}$nce upon a time, there was a beautiful golden flower with magical healing powers. Only a vain and selfish woman named Mother Gothel knew where it grew. For centuries, she used the flower to preserve her youth.

When the Queen of a nearby kingdom fell gravely ill, the whole kingdom searched for the magical flower to help cure her. A palace guard found it and brought it to the Queen at once. After drinking a potion made from the flower, she was magically cured.

Soon the Queen gave birth to a beautiful baby girl. To celebrate, the King and Queen launched a lantern into the sky.

Once she no longer had the magical flower, Mother Gothel aged into an old woman. Furious, she snuck into the castle nursery. She saw that the baby's golden hair glowed and would make her young again.

Mother Gothel scooped up the baby and vanished into the night. She knew that she could only stay young if she always kept the child with her.

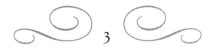

Mother Gothel fled with the child, Rapunzel, and locked her in a secret tower deep within the forest. Though everyone searched for the young princess, they could not find her.

The King and Queen were heartbroken. Each year on their daughter's birthday, they released lanterns into the night sky. They hoped the light would guide their princess home.

Many years passed. Mother Gothel raised Rapunzel as her own daughter. Although she was not allowed out of the tower, Rapunzel grew up to be a bright and spirited girl. And her golden locks grew very long, so long, in fact, that Mother Gothel would call to her to be pulled up the tower from outside.

"Rapunzel, let down your hair."

Rapunzel spent her days painting, knitting, playing the guitar and doing chores. Her only friend was a chameleon named Pascal, but she was happy. She longed for just one thing. On the day before her eighteenth birthday, she decided to take a chance and ask for it.

"I want to see the floating lights!" Rapunzel pointed to her painting of the lights. "They appear every year on my birthday, Mother, only on my birthday. And I can't help but feel like they're . . . they're meant for me."

Mother Gothel was astonished. "You want to go outside?" She told Rapunzel that the outside world was far too scary a place for a weak and helpless girl like her. "Don't ever ask to leave this tower again."

By Order of the KING
WANTED!
1,000 CROWNS REWARD!

THIEF

Meanwhile, in another part of the forest, a thief named Flynn Rider was on the run. He had just stolen something valuable with the help of the Stabbington brothers. Flynn clutched a satchel tightly as he came to a stop in front of a wanted poster of himself. He thought he looked far more handsome in real life!

The palace guards were chasing them. "Retrieve that satchel at any cost!"

As soon as he could, Flynn ditched the Stabbington brothers. They were too dangerous to be trusted.

Next, Flynn dodged boulders and leaped among trees, losing all the guards. But a palace horse named Maximus kept chasing him. They went all the way to the edge of a cliff and onto a tree branch.

The tree broke, and Flynn and Maximus tumbled into the canyon below.

When they landed, Flynn took off. He soon discovered a cave and ducked inside to hide.

He went to another entrance of the cave and spotted an enormous tower in the centre of a hidden valley. He thought it would make the perfect hiding place!

Using two arrows, Flynn scaled the tower and climbed into the open window at the top.

Inside, Rapunzel was startled by the sight of a stranger. She hit Flynn on the head with a frying pan.

Flynn was out cold. Rapunzel dragged him to a cupboard and locked him inside.

She had just defended herself from an outsider! Surely this act of bravery would prove to Mother Gothel that she was strong enough to handle herself in the outside world.

"Rapunzel, let down your hair!" Mother Gothel was on the ground below, having just returned to the tower.

Rapunzel decided to ask Mother Gothel again if she could see the floating lights. She was about to show her the stranger in the cupboard, but Mother Gothel cut her off.

"But if you just –"

"Rapunzel, we're done."

"Oh come on –"

"Enough with the lights, Rapunzel. You are not leaving this tower! EVER!"

Rapunzel was shocked. She decided to convince Mother Gothel to leave on a short journey.

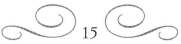

Once Mother Gothel was gone, Rapunzel dragged Flynn
out of the cupboard and offered him a deal. "Tomorrow evening
they will light the night sky with these lanterns. You will act as my
guide, take me to these lanterns, and return me home safely. Then
and only then will I return your satchel to you."

Flynn had no choice. "Fine, I'll take you to see the lanterns."

As much as Rapunzel longed to leave the tower, now that the
time had come, she was terrified. But when she glanced back at her
painting of the floating lights, Rapunzel overcame her fear.

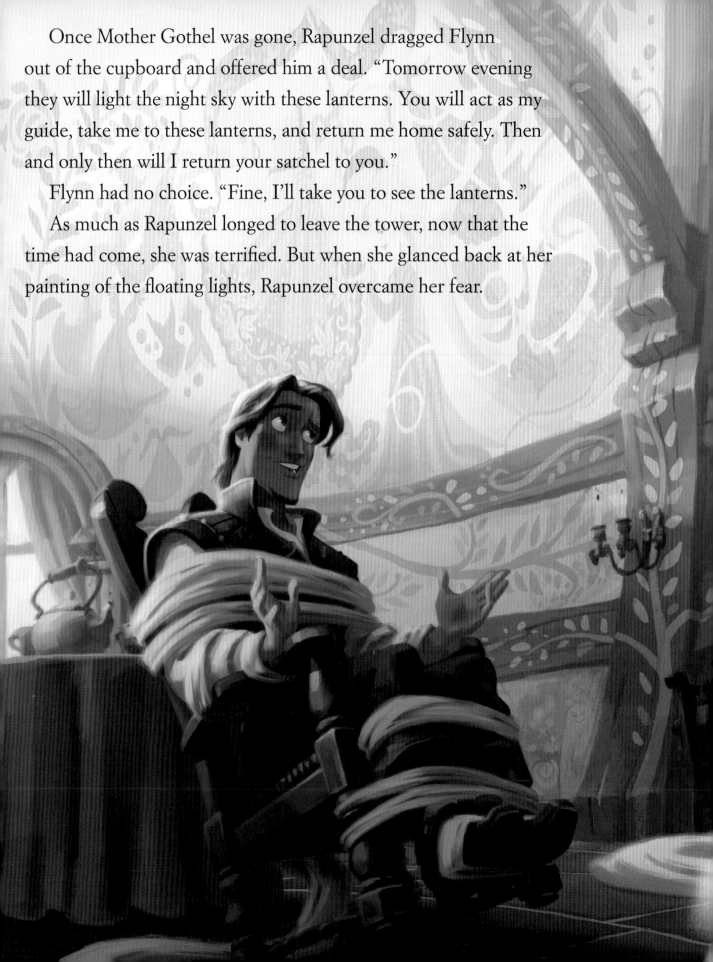

With Pascal on her shoulder, she slid down her seventy feet of hair, stopping just inches above the ground. Slowly, Rapunzel touched one foot to the soft grass, then the other.

"I can't believe I did this! I can't believe I did this! I can't believe I did this!" Rapunzel was having the time of her life. But she also felt like a terrible daughter for lying.

Flynn tried to make her feel even worse. But Rapunzel knew what she wanted. "I am seeing those lanterns."

Not far from the tower, Mother Gothel came face to face with Maximus. She saw the kingdom's sun symbol on his chest. "A palace horse!"

She suddenly realized that the palace guards might have come for Rapunzel! She turned and raced back to the tower. "Rapunzel? Rapunzel, let down your hair!" But there was no answer. Mother Gothel went in a hidden door and searched every room. Rapunzel was gone.

Then she found the crown Flynn had stolen and WANTED poster. She set off to find Rapunzel.

Meanwhile, Flynn took Rapunzel to a tavern filled with thugs so she'd want to return to the tower. Rapunzel was terrified!

Flynn was pleased. "You don't look so good, blondie. Maybe we should get you home . . . call it a day?"

Then someone held up his wanted poster. The pub thugs all wanted the reward money – and that meant catching Flynn.

Rapunzel asked for everyone's attention. "Put him down! I don't know where I am and I need him to take me to see the lanterns because I've been dreaming about them my entire life. Haven't any of you ever had a dream?"

To Rapunzel's surprise, every one of the thugs did have a secret dream. They let Flynn go.

Suddenly, Maximus and the royal guards burst into the pub looking for Flynn. They had brought along the Stabbington brothers, who were now their prisoners. "Where's Rider?"

One of the thugs showed Flynn and Rapunzel a secret passageway so they could escape. "Go live your dream."

Moments later, Maximus discovered where they'd gone. Then the Stabbington brothers broke free and headed down the passageway themselves. They wanted the crown back from Flynn!

Rapunzel used her hair to lasso a rock and swing over to a ledge. She tossed her hair to Flynn, and he swung toward her.

Suddenly a dam burst, and the water began to fill the cavern Rapunzel and Flynn were in. Maximus, the guards, and the Stabbingtons were washed away. Flynn and Rapunzel were trapped.

Flynn searched for a way out. "I can't see anything. It's pitch black down there."

Rapunzel was upset. "This is all my fault. I'm so sorry, Flynn."

"Eugene. My real name is Eugene Fitzherbert. Someone might as well know."

Since they were telling secrets, Rapunzel revealed one of her own. "I have magic hair that glows when I sing."

She realized her hair could save them and began to sing. They dove underwater, and Flynn spotted an escape route!

Meanwhile, Mother Gothel had found her way to the tavern and watched Rapunzel and Flynn escape.

Then she met the Stabbington brothers and offered to help them get revenge on Flynn. With their help, Mother Gothel would trick Rapunzel into coming back to the tower.

By that time, Rapunzel, Flynn and Pascal had made it safely to shore and built a campfire. Flynn had injured his hand, so Rapunzel wrapped her hair around it and began to sing. Her glowing hair healed his wound.

Rapunzel explained that her hair had magic powers that others wanted. "It has to be protected. That's why Mother never let me . . ."

"You never left that tower."

Rapunzel nodded and then changed the subject. "For the record, I like Eugene Fitzherbert much better than Flynn Rider."

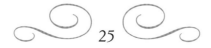

When Flynn went to gather firewood, Mother Gothel appeared from the shadows. "We're going home, Rapunzel. Now." But Rapunzel refused.

"You don't understand. I've been on this incredible journey, and I've seen and learned so much. I even met someone – I think he likes me."

Mother Gothel told her to give the crown to Flynn and then she left. She was sure he would leave Rapunzel once he had it.

Rapunzel wanted to trust Flynn but she was afraid Mother Gothel might be right. She quickly hid the crown.

The next morning, Maximus tried to drag Flynn away!

Rapunzel stopped the horse. "Today is kind of the biggest day of my life. I need you not to get him arrested – just for twenty-four hours. And then you can chase each other to your heart's content. OK?" Maximus and Flynn shook on it.

A bell rang in the distance. Rapunzel followed the sound, and soon the entire kingdom came into view. Her dream was just hours away from coming true!

Flynn, Maximus and Pascal followed
her through the gates of the kingdom.
The hustle and bustle of the town was
the most exciting thing Rapunzel had
ever experienced. A little boy gave
Rapunzel a kingdom flag with the sun
symbol on it.
Then a group of little girls
braided Rapunzel's locks and
pinned them up with flowers.

As Rapunzel continued to walk through the town, she saw a mosaic of the King and Queen holding their baby girl. The Princess had striking green eyes just like Rapunzel's.

Rapunzel and Flynn danced together, visited shops, and enjoyed the sights. As evening approached, they rowed to a spot with a perfect view of the kingdom.

Rapunzel began to worry. If her dream finally came true – then what would happen?

Flynn knew just what to say. "Well, that's the good part, I guess. You get to go find a new dream."

As lanterns filled the sky, Flynn handed Rapunzel her own lantern to send aloft. In return, Rapunzel gave Flynn the crown. She was no longer afraid he would leave her.

Beneath the glow of the lanterns, Rapunzel and Flynn held hands and gazed into each other's eyes.

A moment later Flynn spotted the Stabbington brothers nearby. He turned the boat toward shore. "I'm sorry, there's just something I have to take care of. I'll be right back." He grabbed the satchel and strode off.

Flynn gave the brothers the crown. He'd realized that Rapunzel was more important to him. But they wanted Rapunzel and her magic hair instead!

The brothers knocked Flynn out and sent him into the harbour tied to the helm of a boat. The Stabbingtons told Rapunzel that Flynn had traded her magical hair for the crown. "No, he wouldn't!"

Rapunzel saw Flynn in the boat. It looked like he was sailing away.

Rapunzel ran off into the forest. The Stabbington brothers chased
her. Rapunzel heard a scuffle and found Mother Gothel standing
over the unconscious Stabbingtons.

Rapunzel hugged her. "You were right, Mother."

"I know, darling, I know." Mother Gothel led Rapunzel back
to the tower.

Flynn's boat continued to sail until it crashed into the kingdom's dock. Two guards found him and the stolen crown and dragged him off to prison.

Maximus was nearby. He knew he had to do something.

Inside the prison, Flynn spotted the Stabbingtons in a nearby cell. The brothers admitted that Mother Gothel had told them about Rapunzel's hair and had tricked them so she could get Rapunzel back.

Suddenly, the thugs from the tavern arrived and broke Flynn out of jail! Maximus had planned the entire escape!

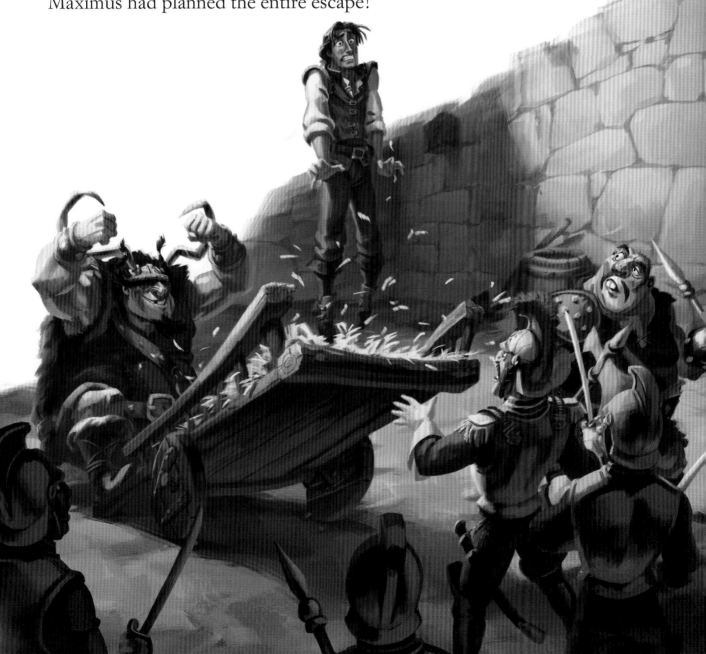

Flynn thanked him, and they went to rescue Rapunzel!

Back at the tower, Rapunzel was heartbroken. She held her souvenir kingdom flag in her hand. As she looked at the sun on the flag and gazed at her paintings, she realized she had been painting the symbol her entire life. She suddenly knew the truth. "I am the lost princess, aren't I?"

Mother Gothel tried to speak, but Rapunzel wouldn't listen. "You were wrong about the world, and I will *never* let you use my hair again." But Mother Gothel wasn't going to let her go.

Flynn soon arrived at the tower. "Rapunzel? Rapunzel, let down your hair!"

The window opened and Rapunzel's golden locks fell to the ground. Flynn began to climb.

When Flynn reached the top, he found Rapunzel chained up. He went to help her, but Mother Gothel wounded him. Rapunzel promised she would stay with Mother Gothel forever if she could heal Flynn. Mother Gothel agreed, but she chained Flynn to the wall.

Rapunzel rushed to him and placed her hair over his wound.

"No, Rapunzel, I can't let you do this."

Flynn mattered more to Rapunzel than anything. "And I can't let you die. It's gonna be all right."

Flynn suddenly reached for a shard of broken glass and cut her hair! It instantly turned brown and lost its magic healing power.

Mother Gothel looked in a broken mirror and saw what she had become: a withered old woman. "What have you done?!" Within moments she turned to dust.

Rapunzel looked at Flynn. "Don't go. Stay with me, Eugene."

He touched her cheek. "You were my new dream."

He closed his eyes, and Rapunzel began to weep. Flynn was gone! A single golden tear fell upon his cheek. Then the tear – and Flynn's entire body – began to glow.

Flynn was healed. "Rapunzel?" The two shared their first kiss.

Flynn, Maximus, Pascal and Rapunzel headed straight to the palace. The King and Queen were thrilled to see their long-lost daughter.

Soon, all the townspeople and Rapunzel's new friends gathered for a grand celebration. Once again, everyone released floating lanterns into the sky. Their light had guided their princess home at last.